D0713530

Ticket to Childhood

Ticket

to Childhood

A NOVEL

Nguyen Nhat Anh

*Translated from the Vietnamese
by William Naythons*

THE OVERLOOK PRESS
NEW YORK, NY

This edition first published in hardcover in the United States in 2014 by
The Overlook Press, Peter Mayer Publishers, Inc.

141 Wooster Street
New York, NY 10012
www.overlookpress.com

For bulk and special sales, please contact sales@overlookny.com,
or write us at the address above.

Library of Congress Cataloging-in-Publication Data
Nguyên, Nhât Ánh, author.
[Cho tôi xin môt vé di tuôi tho. English]
Ticket to childhood / Nguyen Nhat Ahn ; translated from the Vietnamese
by William Naythons. -- First edition.
    pages cm
Novel.
On title page, author's name should read Nguyen Nhat Anh.
ISBN 978-1-4683-0959-1 (alk. paper)
1. Boys--Juvenile fiction. 2. Children--Juvenile fiction. I.
Naythons, William, translator. II. Nguyên, Nhât Ánh. Cho tôi xin môt vé
di tuôi tho. Translation of: III. Title.
PZ90.V5N446413 2014
895.9'2234--dc23
                                      2014034133
Book design and type formatting by Bernard Schleifer
Manufactured in the United States of America

ISBN: 978-1-4683-0959-1
FIRST EDITION
10 9 8 7 6 5 4 3 2 1

"Give me a ticket to childhood . . ."

—ROBERT ROJDESVENSKY

Contents

1. When the day is done

One day, I suddenly realized that life was dull and boring.

The first time this happened, I was eight.

I had the same feeling at fifteen, when I failed my high school entrance exam; at twenty-four, when I got my heart broken; at thirty-three, when I lost my job; and at forty, when I was fully employed and happily married, but then it didn't matter.

There are many shades of boredom, though, and eight was a dark year: I felt that the future had nothing in store for me.

Many years later, I would discover that philosophers had, for millennia, been turning their minds inside out like a pocket looking for the meaning of life, to no avail. But when I was eight, I understood: there was nothing new out there.

The same sun shone every day; the same curtain of darkness dropped every night; the wind in the eaves, and in the trees, moaned the same moans; the same birds sang their same songs; the crickets always chirped the same chirping; and it was true for the chickens squawking the same squawks. In short, all of life was of a sameness: worn out and dull.

Before going to bed every night, I knew for sure what the next day would bring.

Let me tell you: In the morning, I would try my best not to get out of bed. I would pretend to be fast asleep, ignoring my mother's voice and lying there like a log while she shook my shoulders and tickled my feet. Once she roused me, I had to go brush my teeth and wash my face before being forced to sit at the breakfast table, listlessly chewing on something disgusting. My mother's major concern was to make me (and the whole family, for that matter) eat balanced meals, whereas the only food I really liked—instant noodles—she considered junk.

It is good to care about your health, obviously, especially as you get older. Who would deny it? Not me. A journalist once asked me which of humanity's most common cares worried me the most: health, love, or money. Love, I said, was first, and health was second, and money can't buy either, or so they say.

But that's for adults to think about. At eight, I didn't like to eat balanced meals, and was forced to eat them, which I did reluctantly, which is why my mother always complained about me.

After finishing breakfast, I'd hurry to find my schoolbooks and to load my backpack. I'd find one book on top of the TV, another on the refrigerator, and still another buried in a pile of bedding. Of course I'd forget something, as I always did. And then I'd dash out of the house.

I walked to school, because it was near my house, but I never had a chance to enjoy the walk—I always had to run because I always got up late, brushed my teeth late, ate breakfast late, and wasted a lot of time searching for my stuff. Of this cycle my father said: "Son, when I was your age, I always neatly loaded my backpack the night before, so the next morning, I just grabbed it!" I don't know if this was true or not—I obviously wasn't around at the time—but now that I'm my father's age, I say the same thing to my kids. I also boast about hundreds of other sensible things that I also never actually did. Sometimes, for our own reasons, we make up a story about our past, and keep repeating it until we can't remember that we made it up, and if we continue to tell the same story over and over, we end up believing it.

Anyway, as I said, that's adult stuff.

Now back to my story about being eight.

I always took a seat in the back of the

classroom. It was a gloomy spot, but it gave me the chance to chat, argue, or play tricks without fear of being caught by the teacher. But the best thing about sitting in the back was that the teacher never called me to the front to recite a lesson.

How did I get away with this? Think about it: you probably have a lot of friends who aren't on your mind all the time, right? Our memories have limited storage space, like a closet, so the names and faces that don't get a lot of use are stored in the back, where you forget them until you see a familiar face on the street. Then, suddenly, you remember they exist. "Hey, weird—I haven't seen him for ages," you think. "Last year, when I was broke, he lent me a twenty."

Likewise with my teacher: out of sight, out of mind. The thick hedge of dark heads in front of me blocked her view of my face, which obstructed her recall of my name, so she forgot to call on me.

Here's how we referred to school in those

days: *wearing out the seat of your pants*, because we spent so much time sitting on a hard bench. (But let's not be coy—let's call it what it really was: *jail*.) I didn't like a single subject: not math, not calligraphy, not reading, not dictation. I only liked recess.

Who was the adult benefactor that invented recess? What a genius! Recess is an open door. It's an open door in your brain that lets the teacher's droning whoosh out like so much hot air, and it's the door of a cage that frees you to forget your cares.

My friends and I spent those precious moments of freedom playing football or marbles. More often, though, we got our thrills from chasing each other, fighting, or wrestling until the neatly-groomed students who had sat so quietly wearing out their pants looked like a bunch of hooligans with bloody knuckles and black eyes, dressed in their mothers' dishrags.

Maybe you're wondering why, under the circumstances, I don't tell a story about the fun we had after school. That's because there wasn't any. We just went from one form of house arrest to another.

I'm not exaggerating. Every day, when I went home for lunch, I was welcomed at the front gate by the same worried look on my mother's face, the same grimace on my father's.

"Why do you always look like a dead water rat, son?"

Thus spoke my mother.

My father fumed like a dragon: "You got in a fight again?"

"My friends hit me and I hit them back."

When my father took a step toward me with a violent expression, my mother interceded:

"Please don't. He's been beaten up badly enough!"

My mother and I shared a habit of dramatizing things for effect. I followed her into the house, smiling secretly.

After that, as you can probably imagine, my mother would shove me into the bathroom. When I was as clean and fragrant as a bowl of steamed rice, she began to salve my wounds with so much colored goo that I looked like a gecko.

Of course, after that, I was grounded. This meant that I couldn't pick on the little kids in the neighborhood, who made for decent sparring partners when I didn't have my schoolmates to knock around.

What did I do after lunch, when I was eight years old?

Well, I took a nap!

Putting your kid down for a nap is like tying your cow to a post so it doesn't stray or cause damage that would rile the neighbors, who would come over and raise hell. Parents all over the world know this.

In fact, contrary to the common wisdom, naps have no health benefits for eight-year-olds. For old people, yes. With age, your health deteriorates; hard work takes its toll, and a good night's sleep isn't enough to repair all the damage. So it's true, a little nap can help the elderly—that is, people as old as thirty or forty—get back to the workday with a clearer head, so that they don't smash a thumb with a hammer or lose control of their bladder.

But if you have lived on this planet for only eight years, a nap makes no sense. And in some cultures—in America, for example, where people wouldn't think of climbing into bed after lunch—kids aren't forced to nap, either. At least that's what I've heard.

When I was eight, of course, I wasn't thinking in global terms about local customs. I just knew that when my father took a nap, he forced me to take one, too, like the farmer who tethers his cow when he lies down for his own rest. So I lay beside him on the couch, heaving restless sighs at the thought of my friends exchanging punches outside.

"Stop fidgeting! How can you sleep that way?" my father said, and I pretended to obey him. I lay still but my eyes were still open.

"Shut your eyes!" my father added. But how did he know they were open if his own lids were closed?

I tried closing my eyes, but I just succeeded in narrowing them, like the slats of a shutter, because the eyeballs were still moving.

"Are you sleeping yet?" my father asked a little while later. How stupid is that? If I told him I was fast asleep, which I always did, he knew that I wasn't.

I lay like that, bored stiff, and feeling very sorry for myself, until I dozed off without knowing it.

When I woke up, it was back to the old routine: splash some water on my face, march straight to the desk, start my homework.

Sometimes, I was allowed a little outdoor playtime, but only under my mother's attentive gaze (she was inside, spying on me from some secret vantage point I never discovered), and I was limited to sissy games like hopscotch or blind man's bluff. Later, I wised up and figured out how to sweet talk my mother into letting me have "study dates" at my friends' houses. Away from her watch, I could do what I wanted.

After my little break—if I got one—it was back to work. The more I read, the more I forgot, but I nattered on, reciting my lessons like a parrot in order to make my mother confident enough of my diligence to leave me alone and start cooking.

As the evening wore on, my boredom knew no bounds: while the rice was cooking, I wearily memorized page after page. When the rice was ready, I wearily ate it. Then, wearily, I went back to my books. I wasn't allowed to budge until I had memorized all the lessons for the next day.

It was my father who tested me, and unlike my mother, he was so thorough, determined, and unforgiving that he might have had a brilliant career as a policeman, a judge, or a tax official. He was never moved by my fatigue or by my tears, nor did he show any sympathy for the pathetic look on my face—I resembled nothing less than a spent galley slave on the brink of death.

It went like this:

"I'm all done, dad."

He approaches with a suspicious look: "Are you sure?"

"Yes, I'm sure!"

He begins to test me, and I immediately contradict myself by flubbing the very answers that were best rehearsed. How did this happen? Did I bang my head and have a concussion without knowing it?

"Take another go at it, son!" my father commanded, and then he turned back to his newspaper. The aggressive way he rustled its pages as he settled into his chair was a kind of warning: he would read it ten times, if necessary, down to the smallest ad for used tires, while I learned my lessons to his satisfaction. But now the words in my textbook swarmed on the page like enemy soldiers. To memorize them was to defeat them, and they seemed determined to resist me.

You can probably guess the outcome of this battle. By the time I mastered my lesson even just passably, sleep, like quicksand, was dragging me under.

Thus ended one day in my life.

2. Wonderful parents

So there you have a day in my life.

One is enough. There is no need to describe other days, as every day was the same. "A day like any other day," as the saying goes.

Another way to put it is to call my life totally monotonous. The definition of monotony is dull, endless repetition. (*Mono* = one; *tono* = note.)

Only later did I find out that adults take a kinder view of repetition—they call it stability.

A lot of people will tell you that happiness means landing their dream job. Their plans come true—wow, life is great! Maybe it's also great if you can predict a country's economic growth rate.

But wouldn't it be a nightmare if you could also predict your emotional growth rate? Wouldn't it spoil things if you could know, for sure, that in a month's time, you would meet someone special; in three months, fall in love; in six months, get engaged; and so on?

Many young people strategize their future like they're planning an economy: age twenty-two, graduate from college; twenty-five, get married; twenty-seven, get a promotion; thirty, first kid. And so on. What precision! But if you try to live life by clockwork, if everything takes place as if according to a schedule, is there any room left for emotion? Yet I've discovered that one man's boring rut is another man's domestic harmony. It's all a matter of opinion.

I've been off on an adult tangent here, talking about married life. So let me get back to my subject: what happened when I was eight.

But the truth is that the story I'm going to tell *is* related to the business of husbands and wives (a mostly depressing business) if only in the form of a game, one that kids that age love to play, without the caution that they bring to marriage as grownups, when the stakes are real.

I got married to my neighbor Ti, a girl with a missing tooth.

Ti was by no means beautiful. She had wild curly hair, big ears, and a swarthy complexion from her long days in the sun. And the tooth didn't help.

But I was willing to accept Ti as my wife, just because she liked me and obeyed me at all times. To tell the truth, I was in love with Tun, because she was the prettiest girl in the neighborhood, and had adorable dimples. But I didn't marry Tun because I often saw her mooning at a tall boy named Hai, who was a year older than me. I didn't know, at the time, that my feelings about Tun and Hai had a name—jealousy.

I hated them, but you'll see what I did about it.

So, following the advice you always hear from some cynical old aunts and uncles—choose the one who loves you, not the one you love, especially if they don't love you back—I married Ti. And we had been married for about five minutes before we had twins: a son and a daughter. Can you guess their names?

• • •

"Where are you, Hai?" I called in a loud grumpy voice.

"I'm here, dad," Hai answered brightly, and he came running.

"Bring me some water!" I commanded.

(Hai was playing my son, Tun, my daughter.)

Seeing Tun giggle, Hai became stubborn:

"I'm doing my homework."

"Doing your homework?" I shouted. "You slacker!"

Hai gouged out his earwax with a finger so he could hear more clearly:

"Doing homework makes me a slacker?"

"Exactly! Good boys run and jump, climb trees, swim in the river, and get into fights. They don't waste their time on homework."

Hai couldn't believe his father's miraculous derangement.

"Okay, I'll go pick a fight now!"

He ran off, and I was extremely delighted. I had found a way to make life less boring.

"Tun!" I shouted.

"Yes, dad. Want me to bring you some water?"

"Don't get smart with me," I growled. "I'm not thirsty anymore."

Then I made a show of exploding:

"I hate intelligent children who can memorize their lessons in the blink of an eye!"

Tun was confused. She cowered.

"No, no, no. My memory is a sieve. I'm very stupid."

"That's a good daughter then," I said. I

rummaged in my pocket for a piece of candy, stuck there from the day before. "Here's a reward!"

Tun took the candy with surprise. She didn't know why a parent would reward stupidity. Maybe it was a trick. So she didn't dare to eat it.

I was about to tell Tun to eat the candy when Hai rushed into the house, out of breath.

"You've been fighting?" I asked hopefully.

"Yes, dad," Hai replied. "I took on ten boys!"

"Bravo," I said fondly, "but why are your clothes . . ."

"It's okay, dad," Hai replied nervously. "I worked them over, alright, but my clothes . . ."

"You little devil!" I interrupted. "How can you have been in a proper brawl without ruining your clothes or bruising your face?"

Hai looked stunned at my outburst. He didn't know how to react except by stammering:

"Well . . . well . . . but . . . but . . ."

"What do you mean, 'well well, but but?'" I cuffed him on the ear.

My wife was puzzled by my pedagogical methods. "But it was good of him to keep his clothes clean," she said.

"What do *you* know?" I sputtered at her. (I was so angry that spit came out of my mouth, but luckily it missed her eye.) "A fight isn't a tea party! His ancestors would have been ashamed to see him come home from a battle with clean clothes!"

I pounded my chest like an alpha gorilla.

"You might just as well have plunged a dagger into my heart," I told Hai. "So now finish the job: come over here and kill me!"

Terrified by my bellowing, Ti kept quiet.

At that point Hai doubled up with laughter, and now it was Tun's turn to look stunned. She looked, in fact, as if a pigeon had just shat on her face. Her brow was furrowed with perplexity—she'd never seen anyone accused of disgracing his ancestors.

• • •

This was a good trick, but it only caught my friends off guard once—the first time I pulled it.

Then, like any normal kids, my friends got into the game.

The next day, a Sunday, Hai and Tun played the parents, Ti and I the children.

"Where's Little Mui?" Hai shouted.

(Little Mui was my parents' nickname for me. I was born in the year of the Goat, and "mui" means . . . well, you guessed it.)

"I'm here," I replied.

"Show me your notebooks."

I pulled a notebook from my pocket and handed it anxiously to Hai.

After turning a few pages, Hai's face turned red with anger.

"Little Mui!"

"Yes?"

Hai pounded on the table with his fist:

"What kind of student do you call your-self?"

I had barely replied when he threw my notebook through the window.

"You worthless boy! Clean pages? No ink stains? No dog-eared corners? No smears or doodles? You keep your notebook in this condition? What does this tell your teacher about how we've raised you?"

I hadn't expected Hai to be such an excellent schoolmaster.

"Dad, I'm sorry for my mistakes," I said with cheerful contrition. "I'll never again show you a tidy notebook."

From a corner of my eye, I saw Tun and Ti stifling their giggles the way girls do—tee-heeing behind their hands.

"Hey, Toothless Wonder over there! What are you laughing at?" Hai glowered at Ti. "Have you finished cooking? You better have a good excuse for standing there with a stupid grin."

Ti replied respectfully:

"Yes, father, the meal is ready. Would you please come and eat it?"

"Have you lost your mind, daughter?" Hai shouted, "Only fools gather at the table when it's time to eat, do you understand?"

"Then what do educated people do at dinner time?" Ti replied meekly.

"They jump in a lake, play billiards, go fishing, chase one another, get into fights. Generally speaking, they do everything possible to keep their family waiting."

"Your father is right," Tun chimed in primly.

• • •

At first, I thought that only Hai and I loved this game, but it turned out that the girls loved it, too. Ti was the most good-natured of our gang—and the slowest—but on the third day, when it was her turn to play the mother, she really got into it.

"Hai, what is two times four?"

"Eight."

Ti didn't shout the way Hai and I did, but she looked very stern:

"How could it be eight, son? What a disgrace! Haven't we sacrificed for your education?"

"What is it, then?" Hai asked, blinking.

"Anything but eight."

"But mother, the multiplication table says . . ."

"Are you a parrot, son? Do you just dumbly echo multiplication tables? Or maybe all kinds of tables? What is the dining room table telling you? How about the tea cart? Don't you have a brain?"

Hai scratched his head remorsefully:

"I guess I'm just a dolt. Next time, I won't believe anything I read or hear at school."

Hai's promise became our motto, ending a dark period of slavish obedience to the rules of the grownup world.

But, as the saying goes, happiness doesn't last forever.

One day Hai showed up to school looking miserable.

"What's wrong? Did you get a beating?" I asked him.

"Yes. Because I told my parents that only stupid children keep their school books in order."

Then Ti showed up, with a sullen face:

"My father punished me for insisting that three times five wasn't fifteen."

Tun added to the gloom with a stream of tears and a little sniffling.

"I let my mother shout herself hoarse calling me home to lunch."

I glanced at my friends and heaved a deep sigh.

So much for my precocious career as a revolutionary.

But if I wasn't sulking, crying, or looking depressed, it didn't mean that I wasn't suffering. Mine was an internal pain, and it was more acute than all the unhappiness of my playmates put together. First, I hadn't changed the world as I'd hoped to, so I immediately relapsed into boredom. Second, I had gotten my friends in trouble. And third, they had each been punished for a single error. But the day before, I had committed all three, and been beaten thrice over.

3. Naming the world

After taking our beatings in body and mind, we were eventually forced to accept the evidence of reality that appeared on the back of our notebooks, in the form of multiplication tables. If we wanted to rewrite them and make our own, we'd first have to become world-famous mathematicians. As we waited for that day to come (though no one held his breath), Hai, Tun, Ti, and I had to agree, albeit grudgingly, that two times four was eight.

Humbled by our defeat, we became the well-behaved children that our parents wanted us to be. This meant that we now treated our copybooks as we did our teeth—their cleanliness was sacred—and we stopped confusing diligent students with delinquents, and vice versa.

Life was back in its old groove, and I ran the risk of being worn down by its monotony like a vinyl record played over and over with a dull needle. My only thought was: "What should I do now?"

The revolutionary, it turns out, had another battle plan up his sleeve. So I rallied my troops and told them, "From this day forward, we will no longer call a chicken a chicken, a notebook a notebook, or a pen a pen."

"What shall we call them?" asked Tun.

"Anything else!" I replied.

Hai blinked:

"Call a hat an umbrella, or an arm a leg?" he asked.

"Why not?" I snorted. "You can also call your head your ass."

"But why should we do that?" Ti asked.

That year, I hadn't yet learned the five Ws: What, Who, Where, When and Why. "Why" is always the hardest question—and the most important.

All kids tire and embarrass their parents with "why" questions:

Why does thunder follow lightning during a rainstorm?

Why does hair grow from your head and not the soles of your feet?

Why is sugar sweet and salt salty?

Why is blood red and the sky blue?

Why does a stork sleep on one leg?

Why do men have nipples like women if they don't nurse babies?

Why does the earth go around the sun?

All this "why-ning" starts about three or four, then progresses to harder "whys" as a child gets older, until the questions he starts asking are so tricky, so exotic, that only a scientist could answer them. As long as children have asked tough questions, parents have tried to change the subject or have said that the answer has to do with God's will. Or they've gotten angry with their kids when they were really angry with themselves for the gaps in their knowledge.

But questions like "Why was I born?" and "Why do I have to die?" stump even scientists. Here you get into philosophy. Thousands of years ago, an Indian prince named Siddhartha gave up his kingdom, and went into the forest with a begging bowl, looking for answers, hoping that they would, in turn, reveal the truths and mysteries of our human condition, and he became the most enlightened being who has ever lived: the Buddha.

Sorry, I'm rambling. But it's all because of Tun. She asked me "why," and to answer her, I could only do one thing. At eight years old, without the slightest ambition for the job—to say nothing of character—I had to become a philosopher.

"Why?" I responded. "Because we need to reject the arbitrary rules invented by grownups. Why should we call a dog a dog? Because 'a dog is a dog?' If the first man had called a dog a banana, we would now call it a banana. It's just foolish conformity."

"Of all the *bananas* in the neighborhood," Hai chimed in, "Tun's is the most vicious. If she didn't keep it on a leash, I would never set foot in her house even if I were her husband!"

"I think you should close your fat foot!" Tun growled at Hai.

Hai kicked up his foot and frowned:

"I think Ti meant your mouth," Ti said helpfully.

"Ah," Hai bowed solemnly. "From my foot to God's ear."

• • •

In those days, an outsider eavesdropping on us would have thought he had landed on an alien planet.

I'm not kidding. Who could have made block or tackle (head or tail) of the following conversations?

"It's getting dark. I'm going home to fish."

"My mother has promised to buy me a new cloud for my birthday."

("Fish" meant "go to bed," and "cloud" meant "backpack.")

Our parents were exasperated by our Newspeak, especially as the habit gradually got so engrained that when Ti's father told her to turn off the fan, she turned off the TV; and when Tun's mother asked her to buy some bananas, she walked the dog.

At that time, we thought our game was an ingenious invention—the kind of thing that only children could think of. We wanted to rename everything in the universe as if we had just created it. We did this because we were so young, and the world was so old. It was a way of staking our claim to a new, richer dominion of our own.

But when I grew up, I discovered that adults like this game, too, though for a very different reason. They call bribes *gifts,* for example, and speak of corruption as *the cost of doing business.* The purpose of renaming actions or concepts in this way is to muddy what is crystal clear, to use ambiguous language in place of a simple word that nobody could misunderstand. If the adult version of the game gets any more out of hand, the Swedish Academy is likely to award the Nobel Prize for Physics to someone *who can exert hidden force on a stationary object to move it from one place to another without its owner being the wiser:* i.e., to a pick-pocket.

In the real world, though, there is a price for changing the rules.

Take Hai's slip-up.

His teacher called on him to recite a paragraph from his reader.

Hai calmly picked up his *math book*.

"You didn't bring your reader?" the teacher asked, incredulous. "What about your notebook? Did you take notes yesterday?"

Hai pulled out a *hat* tucked in his pocket and put it on the table.

"Is this a joke?" The teacher sprang to her feet and her face went red. "Come with me to the principal's office immediately!"

"Please, Miss. The principal isn't in school today. We had a fight and he is now at home moaning and groaning."

Of course, *the principal*, in Hai's mind, was me. The day before, Hai and I had fought, and I had run a temperature in the evening, God knows why, so my mother kept me home. But Hai boasted that I had taken to my bed because he had beaten me up so badly.

In our alternate universe, Hai was the *Sheriff*, Tun was a *flight attendant*, Ti was *Snow White*, and I was the *Principal*. We re-named ourselves according to our secret desires.

In the days before Hai accidentally betrayed our code, our world was full of chatter like this:

"*Principal*, I am going to set my banana on you if you don't give me my cloud back."

"What's stuffed in your fat foot, *Sheriff*? At the very least, you could share the snack."

"*Snow White*, you stink! Did you wet the bed while you were *fishing* last night?"

"*Flight attendant*, what a cute new knitted *notebook* you have, there. Let me try it on!"

And it was great calling chopsticks *billiard balls*, and mischief *napping*.

Fortunately, after ten minutes of interrogation, the real principal understood that Hai was suffering from temporary insanity. But by the next day, a dog was a dog again, and we were forbidden to rewrite the dictionary. Could it be that the adults reimposed their language on us because they were envious?

4. As sad as sad can be!

Uncle Nhien loves Linh.

I asked Uncle Nhien, "Why do you love Linh?" He didn't reply, and I was surprised at his embarrassment.

Later, when I fell in love for the eighth time, I began to understand that explaining why we don't love someone is much easier than understanding why it is that we love them.

A man, it is said, might marry a girl for her beautiful eyes, but a woman would never marry a guy just because he had great legs. Neither of these is true. Body parts may have a role to play in attraction, but they're like an usher's flashlight. They lead you to a seat in the theatre, but it's the play itself that determines whether or not you stay to see it.

Wait, what am I talking about?

I'm talking about Uncle Nhien.

He loves Linh.

They're a real couple who are getting married.

I didn't know whether the *sheriff* would marry the *flight attendant* when they grew up, but the *principal* wouldn't be stupid enough to marry *Snow White*.

Ti was not on my marriage radar simply because, in terms of cooking, she was the worst.

And as I told you in the first chapter, I was not a picky eater. I didn't care about nutrition. Much later, I did have to care about such things as the percentages of protein, cholesterol, glucose, and lipids in my diet. But when I was eight, I loved only three dishes: instant noodles, instant noodles, and instant noodles. If my mother saw me with a package of instant noodles on the way to the stove, she snatched it away by force, if necessary. This was an assault absolutely contrary to her sweet nature.

In short, if I wanted instant noodles, I had to go to Ti's house and ask her to cook them for me. I call it "cooking" to be polite. Is there any dish in the world as easy as instant noodles? You open the package, dump it into a bowl, add a pinch of salt, then pour in the boiling water. Making an omelet is like launching a spaceship by comparison. Yet even at the advanced age of eight, Ti could never do it properly.

Sometimes, the noodles tasted like a fisherman's rope—tough and salty. At other times, she drowned them the way you might try to drown a cockroach or an unwanted kitten. Once in a while, she got the water right, but then she forgot the salt.

For these reasons, I fired Ti as my instant noodle chef not long after she was hired. I said in a loud voice (my "husband" voice, though we weren't playing):

"Step aside! I'll do it myself!"

• • •

When I was nine, my mother had a baby and I got a sister.

I bring this up because at eight—Ti's age during the noodle debacle—my sister could cook rice and stew fish, clean the house, do the washing-up, and lots of other daily chores.

My mother told her:

"Girls must be able to do everything. When you are grown up, you will get married, and your husband and in-laws will judge how badly or well your mother has raised you by your housekeeping skills."

That is how every traditional Vietnamese mother thinks. So what was wrong with Ti's mother?

Death is what was wrong with her. Yes, sadly, Ti's mother died giving birth to her. Because Ti didn't have a mother, she learned to cook from the worst possible teacher: her father. How they survived is a good question.

Probably by eating a lot of raw food.

Of course, when I was eight, I didn't yet have a younger sister, and my mother hadn't had a chance to express her views on domestic virtue. But even still, I was determined not to marry Ti.

My requirements for a life partner were not terribly demanding. She had to be able to cook instant noodles for me.

As you read this, you must be thinking: "What a jerk!" Maybe you're also thinking, "what century was he born in!" Or, "why didn't he cook his own damn noodles?"

But morally, it's not that simple. For one thing, what people call "modern romance" is an illusion where men are concerned, and that's the truth. Most men still want an old-fashioned wife i.e. a great cook and house-keeper even if they won't admit it. That said, cooking certainly doesn't play a big part in the first stage of romance. Thousands of romance novels are published every year, in every lan-guage, and if you go back a few centuries, there must be millions of them. But how many of their dénouements depend on the girl's cooking? Does a boy ever desert his true love because of her soggy fritters? Romeo ignored a murderous family feud to elope with Juliet, but not because she whipped up a delicious bowl of spaghetti. (Here I have to say, however, that I believe their story is so beautiful precisely because they die before the instant noodle issue comes into play.)

I'm getting to the point, so bear with me. How many boys in our culture get a chance to judge their fiancées' cooking until they have married them?

It's not, as I've said, that the boys don't care about cooking—they do; or that the girls deliberately try to conceal their ineptitude. Eating is just obviously a low priority for lovers. The heart is nobler than the stomach, no? Truong Chi, that legendary antique poet, thought so, at least, and who am I to contradict him?

A boy in love likes to take his girl out to

eat. If he has plenty of money, he takes her to a fancy restaurant. If he's on a budget, he takes her to a café. If he's a poor slob, they squat at plastic tables in a squalid alley eating boiled caterpillars. When his pockets are empty, he tells her that he's "very busy with my work today." What self-respecting Vietnamese boy would ever think of asking his girlfriend to cook for him?

Not until the marriage veil is lifted does the benighted bridegroom give proper consideration to his dilemma—a dilemma he will face three times a day for his whole married life.

Are you with me on this? Would you agree that a marriage can sometimes founder over a bowl of fish sauce? That a perfectly boiled instant noodle not too soft, not too firm, not too salty, not too bland—is sometimes even more important than good relations with your in-laws?

That was what I figured out when I was about forty.

I realized there was an intimate relationship between happiness in the dining room and in the bedroom. You may think me naïve, you may even think I am a Neanderthal, but I was as excited about this belated discovery as Newton must have been when he got conked on the head with the apple. So brace yourself for another revelation: cooking is something that can be improved!

• • •

If we relate my current state of enlightenment to my past decision not to marry Ti, you might be inclined to say that I was mistaken. Why? Because after many years of married life, Ti and her husband are still together, with five kids, all healthy and happy. So, I have to conclude that that they all like raw food.

Now, let's get back to Uncle Nhien and Linh.

Uncle Nhien couldn't explain why he loved Linh. But it didn't prevent him from texting her.

He texted her from his cellphone, and one of the reasons I looked forward to seeing him was the chance to play with it.

But it was a two-way street, because he wanted to see me, too, since I asked him about Linh.

Once I read a message that he sent her:

Shall we go for a short walk this evening? I'm so very sad!

I found this enchanting (though I wasn't sure why), and I ran to Ti's house at once:

"Do you have a cellphone?"

"Of course not, are you crazy?"

Then I ran to Tun's house:

"Do you have a cell?"

"I don't, but my mother has one."

"Borrow it from her," I said. "I will text you after lunch."

Tun looked very pleased. Nobody had ever texted her before.

So after lunch, before being tethered like a cow to the sofa, which is to say, making *mis-*

chief, which is to say, having my *nap*, I borrowed Uncle Nhien's cellphone and texted Tun.

It goes without saying that Tun and I *went for a short walk* together. We just walked around the neighborhood and stood, for a while, by the watercress pond on the side of Hai's house to see grasshoppers jump back and forth; at times, we slapped our thighs because mosquitoes were biting us. But it was fun to do something so adult. It was a "real" date.

A few days later, I sent Tun another text. I copied another message Uncle Nhien had sent Linh:

Shall we have a little drink this evening? I'm so very sad!

And that evening, we met for a little drink at Hai Dot café. I stole some money from my mother to buy Tun a bowl of sweet soup. She cost me (or my mother), but I didn't regret it. Small things like that make life enjoyable.

The third time I texted Tun . . . well, maybe

you can figure out what happened before I tell you.

Once again, I copied one of Uncle Nhien's texts to Linh.

Shall we get into bed together this evening? I'm so very sad!

That evening, I stood at the gate, waiting for Tun as eagerly as before.

A moment later, someone emerged from her doorway: Tun's angry mother. She stormed towards my house.

The upshot was that I got into bed by myself that night.

I lay face down while my father gave me a good spanking you know where.

So very sad!

5. As one grows older

My dear readers, some of you, by now, will have noticed a slight chronological inconsistency in the last chapter. There were no cellphones when I was eight! But authors sometimes have to adjust the facts for the sake of their drama, or their dreams, or to make a point. I also can't be sure that there were instant noodles when I was eight. Were there? Did we have fast food in Vietnam then? I can't remember, even though I claim they were my favorite food. But I'm telling the truth if you play my word game and replace the expression "favorite food" with "favorite comic ploy." *Instant noodles.* Is there anything funnier? You just have to say, "instant noodles," and you burst out laughing. The very sound of "instant noodles" instantly makes life less boring.

And as for what some readers, many of them female, might consider my retrograde ideals of wifely virtue, I have to remind you that just as the Principal wasn't really Little Mui, "I" am just a character. So any offensive opinions that "I" may express may be the views of an old goat.

But here I must also confess that I've been keeping another secret from you.

I intended to keep this a secret, even after I finished the book and it was published. But since you have been patient enough to reach this point, I can find no reason why you shouldn't have the right to the information about the story you have paid for, and invested your time in reading.

Now, I might as well admit that what I'm writing is not a novel. Nor is it a memoir. Nor is it a daydream that I had during one of my siestas.

This is the draft of a paper I intended to

deliver at a workshop with the title, *Children as a World,* organized by UNESCO Vietnam, with the participation of researchers, psychologists, journalists, educators, and writers of children's literature.

Of course this isn't the text that was to have been delivered at the forum. I will tell you the reasons later.

Or maybe I'll just get to it right now.

There are several reasons, each having a specific form.

The first one has the form of Hai.

The name "Hai" just escapes me automatically, and without any honorific, the way it used to when he was nine, my elder by a year.

Now I must call him Mr. Hai, because Hai is eight times six plus 2—i.e. fifty years old, if we have to obey the multiplication table.

One rainy afternoon, Hai—I'll drop the "Mister" for now—came to see me.

He pulled up a chair, and sank into it

heavily before coming to the point of his visit:

"I've heard that you're writing something about our childhood. Is it true?"

"Well, how do you know?"

"You don't need to know how I know. You just need to say if it is true or not."

Hai sounded like a judge, though I knew he ran a company that had nothing to do with legal matters.

"Well, well . . . yes," I stammered.

"So it's true?"

"It is just a—a conference paper," I said, wetting my lips nervously.

"It's not important whether it is a conference paper. People will read it. I want to know what the hell you wrote in it."

"Just some trivial things about our childhood games—"

Hai thrust his hand out.

"Show it to me."

I was going to refuse, but I thought the better of it, because my refusal would only make him more belligerent, so I opened the desk drawer, and handed him the manuscript.

"Read it! There's nothing slanderous in there! Only wonderful childhood memories."

Hai turned the pages, scrutinizing every word, and I had the feeling he was scanning the document, as a computer does, for a nasty virus.

At certain points, he sprang up, paced the room, and shouted at me:

"Brawling and more brawling! Not acceptable!"

Or: "This won't do! I'm a family man! I'm a CEO! You can't describe me like this!"

"Like how?" I asked with fake naivete.

Hai smacked the manuscript on the desk.

"'I'll never again show you a tidy notebook.' Aren't you afraid your teacher will think your parents don't know how to raise their kids? Or here"—Hai stabbed the page as if he were trying to crush a fly—"'Only fools gather at the table when it's time to eat!' . . . You want to kill me, don't you, Mui?" he said, gesticulating the way he used to when we played the husband and wife game.

"This is only a story about eight-year-olds," I said, without much conviction. "And I didn't make things up. I just described you at nine."

"That was then. This is now. Children do countless stupid things. But to make them public is to mock me. What for?"

I couldn't counter Hai's arguments, and I knew I wouldn't be able to win him over. Little Hai was innocent and full of high spirits; Mr. Hai was cunning and narrow-minded.

Little Hai only did what he pleased, as far as he could, while Mr. Hai only wanted to impress others. An adult's life, in that respect, is infinitely more tedious than a child's.

"What do you want, then?" I said eventually.

"Delete all those silly details," Hai demanded.

"No! What would become of my paper? It wouldn't have any life."

"That's none of my business," Hai said coldly.

I took a sip of water to calm down, and put the glass on the desk so as not to throw it against the wall.

"Look!" I told him, "I will not delete or change anything—except the name of your character."

•   •   •

The next day Tun—Madame Tun, to be formal—came to see me and sat on the same chair that Mr. Hai had sat on.

"I've heard that you're writing something about our childhood. Is that true?" she asked.

I nodded mechanically:

"Yes. And I know that as the Headmistress of a prestigious school, it is impossible that, at eight, you ever received a text message from a playmate, inviting you to 'get into bed together this evening.' What would your students and their parents think about you? It would be terrible, right?"

Tun also nodded mechanically.

"So I have decided to change the name of the character. The girl who received that indecent message will be named Hong."

My meeting with Tun ended sweetly.

She didn't ask to read the draft; nor did she wag her finger like a judge. But even if she had been a judge, she would have been pleased with the defendant, who came clean without a whimper, and promised to correct all his mistakes.

6. I am Little Mui

The adult Tun was even prettier than she had been at eight, although now, as then, she didn't love me.

After the texting incident, I had given her a severe scolding:

"Why did you show that message to your mother?"

"Because I didn't understand what you were asking me to do."

"Do you understand it now?"

"I still don't."

"Then never try to."

I said so protectively, because Uncle Nhien had explained the euphemism "getting into bed." As he did so, he laughed at my reactions: first my face turned red, then white, then blue.

In the aftermath of that incident, my father forbade me to use Uncle Nhien's cell-phone. I lost my private channel to Tun, and with it, a secret joy. Life once again became a long, boring corridor with no windows. I came home straight from school, went from bedroom to bathroom to dining table to desk like an automaton—or like a captive planet, revolving around its sun.

Had I been the earth, I sometimes thought, I would have found a way to change my orbit.

But I was not the earth. I was Little Mui.

Still, I managed to make my orbit a lit-tle more erratic. I didn't pour water into a glass any more. I poured it into a soft-drink bottle. We had a carton of them on top of a wardrobe, waiting to be recycled. Swigging from the bottle was sort of fun.

When Hai saw me swigging from the bottle, he ran all the way home to beg his mother for the same drink.

She told him that sodas were just a bunch of toxic chemicals mixed with water, and only crazy people would ingest them.

But Hai found a bottle in the recycling bin.

The next day, he came to my house with a triumphant look.

"Hey! I've been swigging water from this bottle since yesterday."

"What do you think?"

"Water in a bottle tastes sweeter than water in a glass. How strange!"

I also taught Hai other strange things. I stopped eating from a bowl. During a meal, to my parents' surprise, I put my food into a tin wash basin, then carried it to the porch, and squatted there, watching the passing traffic. Life, briefly, was fun again.

Eating from that basin made me look like a pig at its trough, but Hai was intrigued.

The next day, he came to see me.

"I just ate out of a basin," he bragged. "Food in a basin tastes delicious—much more so than food in a bowl. How strange!"

I didn't find it strange—I had foreseen it, but I had no idea why the switch worked.

Now, of course, I understand that our sense of taste is partly based on our expectations—it's psychological, in other words. A change of circumstances leads to a change of feelings.

Why do declarations of love sound more romantic beside a pearly river glowing in the sunset than they do at noon in a crowded marketplace?

Why do couples take "second honeymoons" in faraway places to recover the freshness of their first love?

We need renewal, that's why. New surroundings inspire new perceptions.

And some adults go to extreme measures for the sake of novelty—like quitting a good job, or replacing a spouse. But they don't acknowledge the same needs in their children.

Okay, so Hai and I drank water from a bottle and ate rice from a wash basin, and it didn't change the world. Old wars ended and new ones began. Children still went to bed hungry. Coups deposed this president or that dictator. The Israelis and the Palestinians still fought over their turf.

But from our parents' reactions, you would think that our eccentric new eating habits were something earth-shattering.

"What, are you crazy?" my mother asked. "Everyone drinks water from a glass."

I liked to drink water from a bottle precisely because everyone drank it from a glass. The reason was that simple, but I didn't dare tell her.

My father harrumphed:

"Glasses are used to drink water, bottles are used to hold water, bowls are used to eat rice, and basins are for washing. Don't you know anything, you rascal?"

When my father called me a "rascal," he was really angry.

"Yes, I do."

"Oh you do? Why these whims, then?"

I couldn't explain it all to him, either.

Much later, when I became a real father, not the "father" of Hai and Tun, I found out that kids, as they say, "do the darndest things."

Some don't want to walk normally. They jump or hop or tiptoe, and they prefer teetering on a high wall to planting one foot after the other on solid ground.

Others like to wear their caps backwards.

Still others use their pens as swords, or make boats out of paper, rather than using it for writing letters.

And I'm sure there are kids who drink water from a shell, or even from a shoe, and eat rice from a piece of newspaper, folded into a cone.

And they're very creative, too! They're just making their lives less boring.

Yet adults bristle at any signs of "silliness."

Here is how they see things: you run when you're being chased; you jump when you want to clear a puddle; the brim of a cap is made to protect your face, so it's stupid to wear it backwards. A pen is not a sword—stop waving it around, or you'll put out someone's eye. And good paper is expensive, thank you! You might as well fold up fifty thousand *dong* notes and launch them on a pond.

The objects in an adult's world are defined by their function. Consult a dictionary if you want to know the meaning of adult life. Clothes cover our nakedness; chairs are things to sit on; you eat at a table, and you sleep in a bed. Teeth chew things, and we taste with our tongue.

That's why I don't blame my father for insisting on the "real" function of bowls or glasses.

But kids possess an invaluable treasure—their power to imagine the world differently, and to assign strange functions to familiar things.

For Hai's mother, a broom was a useful construction of wood and straw that she used to sweep her floors. But if I saw Hai standing undecided in front of a broom, I would guess he was thinking about throwing it like a spear, or riding it like a horse, or casting a spell that would make it airborne, like the broom in a fairy tale.

Of course, not all kids resist conformity. They just want to belong. And naturally, adults applaud them for it.

Not that they are wrong to. Standing out in a crowd has always been a risky choice. Just ask the victims of the Spanish Inquisition. (Inquisitions come in many forms.) Like Giordano Bruno—the Roman astronomer burned at the stake for heresy, in 1600, because he believed, contrary to Church teaching, that the earth revolved around the sun.

Hai and I were not burned at the stake.

But we both had to admit that the *function* of children, as adults see it, is to outgrow their childishness.

7. How long can I be a good boy?

So, next question: What else, besides soul-crushing conformity, do adults expect from kids?

Or more specifically, what did my parents expect from me?

I had to wonder, after a series of major setbacks in attitude adjustment.

I didn't think it was all that hard to please them. The real question was: did I want to?

Okay, let's try.

Take One: Humid afternoon; our boring old living room. I get up from the sofa while my father is still snoring away, and I immediately sit down at my desk to study, without waiting for my mother to remind me to, in her habitual tone of timid pleading mixed with commanding urgency.

> *In Vietnamese villages, most people make their living by farming, husbandry, fishing, and handicrafts. Gardens usually surround the houses; there are coops for poultry and enclosures for animals. These rural settlements are ringed by sparsely trafficked dirt paths. In urban areas, most people work in offices, shops, or factories. Houses are crowded together, and streets teem with pedestrians and vehicles.*

Those simple unembellished sentences describe a reality I have seen for myself, and you'd think I could commit them to memory.

But I was a boy with a short attention span. I was always distracted by something else.

I remember the experience of learning the alphabet. The teacher read:

O *is like a chicken's egg*
Ô *is* O *with a hat on, and* Ớ *is* O *with a bushy little whisker*

But instead of concentrating on those helpful images, I thought of Uncle Nhien's hat. It was dark blue, soft and floppy, with a stiff visor, like the circumflex, and made of wool. Nobody wears such a hat these days, but I liked to borrow it and twist it out of shape.

Then my mind wandered to Ti's grandpa. I thought of his beard. Other than its bushiness, it bore no resemblance to the O. It was so long that he had to hold it up, daintily, with one hand, like a Victorian lady lifting her skirt, to keep it out of his soup.

So I was lost in the byways of my free associations when the teacher pointed at the letter Ớ and asked me to pronounce it.

"Well, this is the letter . . . the letter . . ." I stammered.

I knew the letter in question was either Ô or Ơ, but I couldn't say for sure. The images of Uncle Nhien and Ti's grandpa kept running through my mind, but I confused them. Seeing how embarrassed I was, the teacher said sympathetically:

O *is round like a chicken egg*
Ô *is* O *with a hat on, which letter has a* *whisker?*

"It is the letter Ơ, teacher!" I answered, overjoyed.

A wise man once remarked that every letter is like a human face. The first thing you must do in grade school is to get familiar with these faces, then remember their features, as you would with a group of friends who will keep you company for your whole life.

It's not a lot to ask, except of a dreamer like me.

Instead of becoming more familiar as I stared at them, the letters kept dissolving into a crowd of strangers whom I couldn't recognize.

Years later, I stumbled upon *The Vowels,* a poem by Arthur Rimbaud, and I understood that he, too, had been led astray by his imagination:

A black, E white, I red, O blue, U green: vowels.

Not only did Rimbaud assign colors to the vowels, but he also saw a velvety black swarm of flies in the letter A; a vaporous whiteness—of clouds and sails—in the letter E; and idyllic green pastures, dotted with cattle, in the letter U.

More wonderfully, each letter had a sound for him: a brassy trumpet in the letter O; a voluptuous hissing in the letter U; soulful keening in the letter I.

Rimbaud quickly became my favorite poet.

I didn't know much about him—that, for example, he was a teenager when he wrote some of the masterpieces of French literature—

but I figured that Rimbaud must have had the temperament of a rebel; the mind of a dreamer; and the grades of a problem child, just as I did.

But I'm straying from the point again.

My ramblings thus far simply reinforce the point that at the age of eight, I was a boy with muddled thinking.

But I also want to say that one day, just like that, I stopped letting my mind wander, simply to prove that I could.

Now, suddenly, I mastered my lessons in a demonic frenzy. I buried myself in books, forgetting to eat, disdaining play, ignoring Hai and Tun, and Ti's desperate knocking at my door.

I memorized my lessons as if my life depended on it.

I digested the words as avidly as instant noodles.

I recited my lessons out loud until I knew them all by heart.

And by dinnertime, I felt full—as if I had gulped down a stack of books.

Hearing me rattle off chapter and verse

with complete fluency, my father rubbed his eyes, as at a miracle, and heaped praise on me. With a little less self-control, he might even have hugged me.

"Incredible!" he said, stifling sobs of pride.

But my mother was alarmed at the radical change in my behavior.

"Are you ill, son?" she asked, touching her cool palm to my forehead. "Perhaps you need to see the doctor!"

•   •   •

During that period of my transformation from a slacker into a nerd, my teacher started palpating my skull.

She started at the crown, with all ten fingers, going inch by inch, like a doctor checking for a tumor.

"Did you have a fall, recently?" she asked me.

"Yes, I did," I replied. (I had been wrestling with Hai.)

"Did your head hit the ground?"

"Yes."

She applied pressure with her thumbs in a circular, trepanning motion, as if she intended to drill a hole through my temples.

"How did you fall?" she continued. "On the front or on the back?"

"The back, as I recall."

It might have been the back—who knows?—but it also might have been my left ear, or my forehead. When I wrestled with Hai, I crashed in every direction.

"Thank goodness!" she exclaimed. "Then you missed the nerve center!"

My classmates regarded me like some kind of monster who had suddenly sprouted an extra nose, but they were in awe of me, too.

Little Mui, always last, the class clown, was now getting the highest marks, and for the first time, I saw the perks of being a star— my success inspired the laughter of Trang the Flirt.

Trang wasn't a beauty. She was stuck up

and pretentious. But her laughter enchanted me. It sounded like music—the voice of a siren. Whenever she laughed, I couldn't help turning in her direction.

To be honest, I still liked Tun better than Trang—I'm a sucker for dimples. But Tun did have one serious defect—her attraction to Hai. Thanks to Uncle Nhien's cellphone, we'd had our two "dates," but after the debacle with the "getting into bed" business, she went back to Hai, and I was crushed.

So just as I had decided to focus on my studies, I decided not to care about Tun. I would ask Trang to *go for a little walk*, and *have a little drink,* and make sure that Tun saw us—and her feelings would be hurt!

I got this idea while I was jealous, but quickly lost my enthusiasm for it.

After several love affairs, I have learned that you can't embark on a new romance while the injury to your heart from a failed one is still fresh. It's like starting a war while the ruins of a lost battle are still smoldering.

The wounds of love and war both need time to heal.

• • •

This whole intrigue began to bore me—Trang's laughter included.

Ditto, getting the best grades—once you have met a challenge, it ceases to motivate you. Excellence became as tiresome as mediocrity.

I neglected my studies, and once again reduced my father to tears—this time, bitter ones. My mother was worried. (When wasn't she, though?) And my teacher wondered if—freakishly—the nerve center of my brain wasn't in my forehead, where most people have it, but in the back. (That would have explained a lot.)

Only Hai, Ti, and Tun were happy about my work going downhill. In their eyes, my decision to renounce glory for ignominy was the selfless act of a high official who gives up his

villa, his medals, and his motorcade, and be-
comes a monk. It depends how you define a
hero. Heroism is different for kids and for
adults.

8. How we became killers

As I said, there are several reasons why the draft of the paper that you're reading will never be delivered at the UNESCO forum.

The first reason is called Hai.

The second reason is called Tun.

The third reason, of course, is called Ti.

"The third reason" visited me on a beautiful Sunday morning.

She still had a missing tooth.

"Why don't you get an implant, Ti?"

"I like my looks the way they are."

"I think it's your husband who likes them."

"You're right." Her smile was ironic, but its light was girlish.

At eight, Ti was nice, but slow-witted,

and inarticulate. Now, I realized I had mis-judged her.

There are lots of intelligent people in the world, and lots of honest people. As a rule, the super-smart ones are glib and self-serving, while the congenitally honest tend to be sim-ple-minded. What a pity for civilization.

Yet Ti was a special case. She was both honest and intelligent.

She spoke her mind without playing games.

She was devoid of ulterior motives.

Her simplicity was a reflection of her goodness.

"Did you come here because of my writ-ing?" I asked her.

"Yes, exactly," she answered.

"So you must know that I've decided to change the names of the characters?"

"I've come because of that," she said.

"You can rest assured that there's no girl named Ti with a missing tooth in my story."

"That's not why I'm here."

"You don't want me to shred my paper?"

"Shred it? Hardly!" Ti said with vehemence.

"So you want me to shred it and eat it?"

She squirmed with discomfort.

"How about burning it then?" Now I was working up a lather.

"Please!" She implored. An opaline tear formed at the corner of each eye and left a track, like a snail's slime, on her weather-worn cheeks. "I've come to beg you not to listen to Hai and Tun. Tell the truth about our childhood."

I stared at Ti, flabbergasted. What a dolt I was. Forty years ago, this loving creature had been my "wife," and I'd never appreciated her. Now she was middle-aged, with five children, and I deserved a sharp knock on the head.

"I'm sorry—" I said. "I'm sorry for everything." How lame was that?

"The best apology is to take my advice," Ti answered.

Moist eyes are beautiful, no matter how squinty they look dry.

• • •

My interview with Ti reminded me of how I had treated her forty years earlier.

I shouted at her every day just to enjoy her timid compliance with my orders.

One day, to relieve my ennui, I told her:

"Let's go on a treasure hunt."

"Where can we find a treasure?"

"We'll cross the sea. Treasure is usually buried on desert islands."

"But we're so little. How can we cross the sea?"

"You wimp!" I retorted. "Haven't you ever been to the movies? We'll build a raft out of bamboo."

"People who build rafts are adults."

I shrugged:

"Age doesn't matter. Guts matter. Do you have them or not?"

"But adults don't have to ask their parents for permission."

Ti's objection cut me short. I couldn't rebut it. (I guess her intelligent honesty was manifest even then, but I missed it.)

"Fine!" I conceded grudgingly. "No raft, then. But we can search for treasure in the jungle or the mountains."

"Going into the jungle or up in the mountains amounts to the same thing," Ti said, with a little wince of apology for shooting me down again. "Our parents surely won't allow it."

"Our parents never trust us," I said sullenly. "They're always afraid we'll get lost."

My anger was mounting.

"They're afraid of us getting eaten by sharks or tigers."

Perceiving my dejection, Ti became sad, too.

"Just wait 'til we grow up," she said tenderly, patting my arm. "We'll go anywhere we want without anyone stopping us."

Once again, Ti was the voice of reason.

But the truth, as I discovered, is that the freedom of adulthood is oppressive in a different way. You can do anything, so rebellion has no meaning.

Adults, of course, have their own parental authorities. Moral principles are their mothers, rules of law are their fathers. One parent cajoles and induces guilt, the other threatens and imposes punishment. Like kids, though, adults aren't always obedient. That's why religion was invented. People need a higher power.

Well, I've been digressing again!

I was talking about my treasure hunt with Ti.

Of course we never embarked for an island, nor explored the jungle. When I looked at her, I saw a tiny creature paddling in a vast ocean of helplessness, and I realized we were in the same boat.

But as I considered my limited options for adventure, I suddenly remembered the small garden behind Hai's house.

"Hey, Ti," I said brightly, "I've got an idea! People sometimes bury treasure in a garden!"

"A garden?" she echoed.

"Yes, a garden. Just look over there! You see the plum trees behind Hai's house?"

Ti looked vaguely in that direction and squinted.

"Yes, I see plum trees."

"I bet there's a buried treasure there." My voice was firmer than the conviction it expressed.

"Who would have buried it?" Ti asked sensibly.

"Don't be silly—an ancient warrior. Or a pirate. Maybe an exiled king."

"Let's dig it up, then!"

Ti encouraged me, though not because she believed there was pirate gold or a king's ransom under the plums. It got her off the hook for the desert island and the jungle. She could stay home, without upsetting her parents, avoiding—or at least postponing—some act of folly that she was sure

I would, eventually, compel her to carry out.

•   •   •

The excavation crew consisted of our gang of four. We shared everything in life: our joys and sorrows; our beatings and our rewards; the boredom of school, which we bore stoically, as donkeys carry their loads. And we would share the treasure.

We chose a sunny day to begin digging.

Hai's parents made no objection. They thought we had suddenly developed a wholesome interest in horticulture.

"Bravo, boy," Hai's father said, tousling my hair.

Hai's mother teared up when she saw Tun lugging a water bucket: "Be careful, child, or you'll stub a toe!

After a week, there wasn't an inch of ground that was left unturned. Like archeologists, we worked horizontally first, then vertically. We dug carefully under every tree and bush. But treasure was nowhere to be found. In vain, we waited for the telltale clang of a spade hitting wood or metal. Once in a while, we felt a surge of excitement when we felt something hard in the loam, but it always turned out to be a shard of pottery or a rusty piece of iron.

Ten days after we had begun, the poor little garden was as pocked with holes as the moon's surface. Then the trees started dying; the branches drooped, and the plums shriveled up.

The next morning, Hai's father didn't stop to tousle my hair. He pointed at the front gate, like an angry God throwing Adam out of Eden, and told me to get lost.

Hai's mother just moaned.

"The killers! The killers!"

We hadn't meant any harm, yet we had murdered the trees, and we had almost done in Hai's mother.

So Tun, Ti, and I beat a hasty retreat, leaving Hai behind, as he had nowhere else to go. A child's home is like a rabbit's skin—how can he slough it? Only adults have that power of self-transformation. In some cases (though not many, it's true) they reinvent themselves. Or at least that's what I've read.

9. Does anybody have the time?

The next day, Hai came to see me.

I guessed from his angry look that he was about to curse me for destroying his family's garden.

But when he saw my face, his anger disappeared.

"You got a beating too?"

He said it with a little smirk that betrayed the satisfaction of someone in trouble comforted by seeing someone in worse trouble.

"Obviously," I said, touching a swollen cheek. "Your father was here last night. Majorly pissed off."

"Uh-oh," said Hai. "I bet it wasn't his only stop."

As if on cue, Tun and Ti appeared a few minutes later. Their faces were creased like linens just off a clothesline.

Hai and I didn't need to ask why they had been crying.

"What did we do wrong?" I whinnied, in an injured tone.

"You trashed my garden," Hai said.

I appealed to Ti:

"We didn't mean to, did we, Ti?"

"No! And we were so careful!"

Tun was on my side, too, as she naturally would have been—she was an accomplice to the crime.

"Nobody meant any harm," she said.

Hai realized he was outnumbered, so he just sighed.

I still secretly believed that if Hai's parents hadn't driven us away, we would sooner or later have found something. That's how kids think: that somewhere in the world is a hidden treasure just waiting for them to discover it.

Adults usually indulge kids in that fantasy—up to a point. For example, they will smile knowingly and say, "You are so right! There is buried treasure everywhere—the treasure of knowledge!" Knowledge Schmoledge: treasure to an eight-year-old is a chest full of gold coins, or at least a stamp collection, a dagger with a jeweled hilt, some gaudy rings, old swords and muskets—that sort of thing.

"Our parents buy lottery tickets," I protested. That's treasure hunting—and about as likely to produce results as digging under a plum tree. So why were we punished?"

"Why are they never punished for anything?" Tun sniveled.

"My mother has lost the keys to her scooter five times," Hai said, "and nobody says a word."

"My father keeps promising to quit drinking, but he never does!" Ti objected.

Carried away by a flood of resentment, the four of us took turns listing our parents' faults, and in a few minutes, they had mounted up to an impressive indictment of adult folly. You will forgive my hypocrisy (if you are a parent, that is) when I confess that I tell my own kids that I am the judge of their behavior, but they don't dare judge mine—father knows best!

The truth is: what mortal, child or adult, is without error? And who doesn't try to cover his mistakes?

But the deck is always stacked, and you know how. If a kid farts at the dinner table, he will get a slap, but if a grownup farts, everybody laughs it off—the kid first of all.

And not only are kids punished for any little infraction, they are also punished unjustly. If the cat breaks a saucer, if your sister started it, if the dog ate your homework, if your father mislaid his pen, if grandma left the gas on, if the baby fell off the bed, and if Uncle forgot to flush . . . guess who gets blamed! In their impatience to punish the culprit, they never give you time to explain, and they don't believe your excuses, anyway!

People talk about the income gap between rich and poor, but what gap is harder to close than the justice gap between children and adults!

That gap had never yawned greater than it did on the rainy morning when the four of us huddled in my living room, Hai and I with bruised faces, Tun and Ti with circles under their eyes, drawing up the indictment of our progenitors. The next step was obvious: a trial!

After a brief power struggle, Hai and Tun won the role of the judges. (He argued that he was the eldest; she argued that she was the fairest. Ti never argued, and I couldn't win on either count.)

So Ti and I had to play the defendants.

Hai pounded on the table with a wooden spoon. "This court will now come to order! Defendants please rise! You, sir," he said to me, snarling, but using the proper honorific.

"Do you know how late it is? Where have you been all night?"

In the role of Ti's father, I mumbled an apology. "Well, I met a colleague from the office, we got carried away discussing business, we had a few drinks, and one thing . . ."

"Last week, you 'had a few drinks,' as you put it. You rode your scooter straight into a tree, and you wound up at the emergency room. Is that not correct?"

It was all true: everyone thought that Ti's father was a goner, but all he needed were a few stitches, and he was back at work the next day.

I enunciated very slowly, the way drunks do when they're trying to sound sober. I was getting into it. "I do remember it, Your Honor."

"Then why are you drunk again today? If you kick the bucket, who will support your daughter? Losing one parent is bad enough, but losing two is"—he searched for a suitably horrific word—"unacceptably careless!"

I bowed my head, and groveled:

"I know I was wrong."

Hai looked at me fiercely:

"I've heard that before."

Now Tun fixed her steely gaze on poor Ti.

"Madam," she said. "You stand accused of insulting your daughter!"

"That's not true!" Ti cried. "I have always loved her!"

"The other day, you took her shopping, is that correct?"

"Yes, we went to the Chinese market."

"And you were considering two cotton blouses, am I right?"

"Yes, one was yellow, with white polka dots, and one was blue, with a ruffled collar."

"And your daughter liked, nay loved, the yellow one—please correct me if I'm wrong."

"But, but . . ."

"Yet you told her that the blue one was

'much nicer;' that 'yellow showed the dirt,' and so forth. You completely ignored her taste and feelings in the matter, and bought the one you liked yourself!"

Ti, in a blue blouse, started giggling.

"Madam, this is no laughing matter, I assure you! And we are not only speaking of a single shopping trip, are we Madam? You have deprived your daughter of her free will not only in the matter of the blouse in question, but when it comes to socks!" (We were now all cracked up, except for Tun, who was keeping a straight face.) "And not only socks . . . even underpants! The most intimate decision a girl can make!"

"I'm sor—sor . . . ry, Your Honor," Ti managed to gasp, doubled over with guffaws.

The trial lasted several hours. We got our resentments out of our systems. It was like a great purge. Regrettably, though, our joy and triumph were ephemeral. Later that evening, when I walked Hai home, we were met at the door by his father.

"Where have you been?" he shouted at Hai. "Why are you home so late? Do you know what time it is?"

10. And I have sunk

Hai and Tun now flatly denied that any such trial had ever taken place. Commit such a sacrilege? Not Mr. Hai, the CEO, nor Madam Tun, the Headmistress! But Ti and I had not only been the defendants—we were the witnesses!

Retrieving these images from the closet of my memory, I feel a pleasant wave of nostalgia. It is like finding some precious souvenir from a happy trip that's been stored for years on a top shelf and suddenly turns up in a spring cleaning.

But even though I have forgotten many scenes from my past, I have tried, as an adult, to see myself through a child's eyes: not perfect, in other words; not always conscious of myself; a little ridiculous, maybe—like a man unaware of his open fly.

In fact, our personality needs the corrective of a little comic humbling, from time to time. "Hey, Mister, the cucumber has left the salad . . ." Many adults pay more attention to the tidiness of their appearance than to the zippers of their character, which, carelessly left open, expose its faults. But they are less observant of themselves, in this respect, than children are of them. Or they close ranks in embarrassment, and pretend not to notice.

The way that Hai and Tun dealt with their embarrassment at my paper—the unzipping of our childhood—is a case in point. All children are poets, who hear the music and see the colors of letters on a page—magic portals to a wilderness without fixed meanings, where intuition shows you the way. All that adults see are the neat rows of black lines, the building blocks of definitions. And Hai and Tun would have censored my paper with the ink of reason.

Another metaphor: Adults like to keep the cobwebs out of their attics—to clean up the past, as Hai and Tun tried to do. But when you brush those cobwebs away, you may—as Ti perceived so astutely—be brushing off diamond dust.

Well, what I have been writing is now no longer a scholarly treatise on children for an international science workshop. A treatise must be sober and factual—written with the ink of reason. But a work of fiction has no such constraints. So let me add a disclaimer here: "Any resemblance to persons living or dead is entirely (or almost) coincidental."

And let me add a further disclaimer: there was never an eight-year-old boy in Vietnam who asked an eight-year-old girl to "get into bed" with him. Four children never once tried their parents in absentia for crimes against intuition. A lovely little garden of plum trees (they were actually pretty sorry to begin with) was never destroyed in a search for buried treasure. A foot was never a mouth, a hat was never a notebook, and no one ate rice from a wash basin. UNESCO can get on with its important work without worrying about a worldwide epidemic of childhood boredom.

I'm not afraid, now, of how Hai and Tun will react when they read this. I am afraid, however, what my parents will think. And not only them, but all the parents in the world. I'm afraid they may see themselves as the mothers and fathers in the story. But I'm also hopeful that if this tale disillusions them about their model children, it will also remind them that they, too, were once less than model children. And, after all, we turned out all right: A CEO, a Headmistress, a writer, and a mother of five with a husband who loves her missing tooth.

But if the parents who read this are disillusioned, the kids who read it may be, too—and that was intentional on my part. Yes, children, knowledge is a real treasure, but don't confuse, as parents do, *knowledge* with *degrees*. And when you hear grownups talking about love, remember my own mistake: it's not about dimples, or instant noodles.

My daughter no longer asks me why men have nipples, or why thunder follows lightning, or why blood is red, and the sky is blue. But some of her questions are hard to answer.

"They say that marriage is the grave of love. Is that true, dad?"

I thought of Ti's happy marriage, and of others, less successful. "It's only a grave," I replied, "if two people dig it. Marriage teaches you to love, but like anything worth learning, you have to work at it. And lazy students may find themselves expelled."

• • •

I was not lazy, but I still suffered an expulsion.

I remember the day that Tun moved away. Her father got a good job in the city, and the family followed him.

A day before she left, I took the risk of borrowing Uncle Nhien's cellphone and texted her:

Shall we meet to say goodbye this evening? I'm so very sad!

"Little Mui wants to see you," Tun's mother told her. She wasn't angry with me anymore.

So Little Mui and Tun drank some sweet soup together, at the Hai Dot café. A breeze was blowing off the river, and it was the first time that I felt what I now know is adult sadness.

Many people are afraid of sadness, but I'm not one of them. I'm only afraid of boredom. Sadness, in that respect, is an excellent remedy, since it expands to fill almost any void.

When I fell in love, sadness was the subject of my first verses:

Since I made friends with you,
I have known what sadness is
And sadness has also known me
If sadness comes tomorrow
It will just knock at the door of a friend's house . . .

So, sadness rang my bell on the day that Tun left.

I was watching her spooning soup into her mouth, focused on eating. She ate three bowls in a row. Later I found out that girls often eat when they are sad, though a newly divorced man I know told me the same thing: "food fills the emptiness in my heart."

But when she had finished her three bowls of soup, she began to weep. She had eaten three times more than I did, and now she cried six times more. Her face was as wet as if she had been sitting in the rain.

Then she glanced at me rapidly and ran outside.

And that was all there was: eating and weeping. Neither of us spoke a word.

Ten years later, I met Tun again when I came to the city for college. (Hai was already there; Ti was my classmate.)

The four of us had many happy reunions over the years. But I never told Tun how much I had loved her as a child.

Another ten years elapsed—we were both twenty-eight, and Tun was about to get married—when I confessed the feelings I'd once had for her.

"I liked you too," she said calmly.

"Then why did you go with Hai?"

"Because I felt too much for you," she answered.

Tun's confession left me stupefied. I couldn't lift myself from the chair until long after she was gone—leaving a wedding invitation on the table.

Can a boy of eight understand a girl? Can a man pushing thirty understand a woman? And does anyone in love understand himself?

11. Wild dog camp

The soul at birth is like a lake whose surface is unruffled until life skips the first pebble of sorrow across it.

Great, now you know, and I can change the subject to something lighter: raising wild dogs.

This was the project that Hai, Ti and I got into after Tun left, when we noticed that our town was full of strays. Some of them teamed up in packs, the way homeless children do.

One them hung around my house, and I started feeding it scraps. Then I said to Hai and Ti:

"We'll start a wild dog farm."

"What for?" Ti asked, flabbergasted.

"We'll train them to obey us."

"What for?" Hai insisted.

"To sell them, you idiot, we'll make piles of money!"

Financial independence from grownups is every child's dream.

Our farm was based at Ti's house, which was bigger then Hai's or mine. Also, her father was out almost all day.

Hai and I were in charge of the training, though we fought over it, until Ti suggested, ever sensible, that we take turns.

Hai was working with an ugly little mutt whose improbable name was Prince.

He threw a shoe across the living room, and ordered Prince to fetch it.

"Great! Now bring it to me!" Hai shouted, when Prince pounced on the shoe.

But the mutt pretended to be deaf, and ran straight out of the house.

Five minutes later, Hai had recovered Prince and tried again, but this time without shouting.

"Bring it here," he whispered softly.

Prince hesitated for a moment, dropped the shoe, and obediently trotted back.

This went on for a while. Ti and I were hysterical.

"Watch me," I said, "If you want to be a successful trainer, you have to use bribery. Whether it's a dog, a dolphin, or a big cat, tamers always reward obedience with a treat."

I asked Ti to break a rice cake into small pieces.

"Listen, you little mutt!" I told him. "If you bring me the shoe, you'll get a delicious cracker."

Prince was salivating—he understood the cracker part, all right.

"No shoe, no cracker!" I admonished him.

Prince still didn't get it. Or he was making fun of me.

Hai also made fun of me:

"Teaching Prince to disobey is really simple. Even Ti could do it, I bet!"

"Okay, maybe we have to teach by example," I conceded.

So I got down on all fours, Ti threw the shoe across the room, and I crawled over to it. I started to pick it up in my hand—it was filthy—but I figured that wouldn't help Prince get the concept, so, suppressing my gag reflex, I mouthed it. Meanwhile, though, Prince had managed to gobble up the cracker.

"What sort of student are you?" I yelled at him. "*You* are the dog. *I* am the human.

I chased Prince around the room, rabidly, but he escaped, and thus ended our first training session at the dog farm.

The following week, we didn't make any progress, except at enraging our parents.

When all their leftovers began disappearing, Hai's mother got suspicious, as did mine.

When they found out that we were raising wild dogs at Ti's house, our fathers went berserk.

"I will cut your hands off if you continue

stealing food," my father threatened me. Hai's father must have threatened him with the same measure. All he brought to the table, so to speak, were globs of burnt rice.

Oddly enough, the one parent whose outrage would have been justified was very calm. Ti's father didn't utter a word of complaint, and Hai and I were so impressed by his magnanimity that we began to think of him as an enlightened being. That opinion was revised when we noticed that the dogs at the farm kept disappearing.

At first, we thought they had managed to escape the pen we had rigged, inexpertly, out of scavenged chicken wire. But then Ti caught her father and Hai's father drinking at old Ba Duc's pub. As she watched in horror, Ba Duc emerged from the kitchen with a steaming tray of . . . Avert your eyes, children. Yes, that's what had happened to our dogs. They wound up on the barbecue. What a world full of grief.

So the dog camp folded, and our money-making schemes collapsed with it. It was lucky for Ti's father that Tun had moved away—we would surely have tried him for his bestial treachery.

12. Train without a conductor

Many Asians find dog meat delicious. Some allege that it's the favorite food in South Korea. And that's why a lot of Western celebrities objected when South Korea was chosen to host the 2002 World Cup: canine rights.

People in the West are horrified at the thought of eating dogs. Their priorities, I have heard, are as follows: children, women, pets, husbands.

Within a kilometer of my house, there are at least five restaurants serving exotic meats—not only dog (that's not exotic here) but weasel, snake, anteater, porcupine, lizard and ostrich.

I've tried a few, from time to time, but I still prefer beef, pork and chicken. After millennia of culinary experiments, in which our ancestors ingested any sort of wild protein they could find—from frogs to mammoths—they decided that domesticated meat from cattle, pigs, and hens was superior in taste and tenderness, if not lowest in cholesterol. (If dinner is grazing, rooting, or pecking in your backyard, it's also easier to catch.)

And yes, people eat dogs. But to a child, ingesting dog meat seems as barbaric and repulsive as cannibalizing your best friend.

Closing the farm was a painful decision, but what else could we do? With heavy hearts, Hai, Ti, and I carried each dog in our arms to a place by the river where we figured they could scavenge from the fishing boats and the dump. We turned home in sorrow—only to realize, when we got back to Ti's, that those sly mutts had followed us! Against her instincts, therefore, kind-hearted Ti locked her front gate and felt wretched every time she looked up from the table or the TV and saw those sad canine eyes staring yearningly at her lighted windows.

The day the last dog slunk away, its tail between its legs, was the saddest day of our lives.

• • •

Tun's departure, followed by the dog farm fiasco, was too much loss to take. It was, in a way, the end of my childhood. I became pensive, and napping no longer seemed like a punishment. I lost my enthusiasm for changing the world. I had railed at my helplessness, but now I surrendered to it. Adults, I realized, tend to avoid life's uncharted waters and paddle along in shallow manmade canals, just like vehicles obeying traffic rules. And it's all for the sake of safety.

Adults have their good qualities, of course. Now that I am one, I can say so. I'm even proud of my responsible "adult" behavior. And children have their blind spots. They take parental love for granted. (The kids who complain the loudest are often the ones who are loved the best. It takes a certain security to be critical. But I'm philosophizing again.)

Two days after this story was published, I was shaken to see a familiar car pull up at my door. It was Hai's car, and at first I imagined he had come to quarrel with me. But then Tun got out. Each one carried an armload of books.

"Huh? Hey? What? Why . . ." I was at a loss for words.

But Hai was grinning broadly:

"We've come to congratulate you," he said.

I looked stupidly at their piles of books—my book, I realized!

"What's all this?" I asked.

"What do you think? We've bought a carload of these, and we want your autograph."

I still didn't get it. "So you're not angry with me?"

"Why should we be angry?" Tun asked

coyly.

"You blockhead!" Hai cried in a booming voice. "We ganged up on you to stop you wasting a beautiful story on a boring conference paper that no one outside the lecture hall would read!"

"You don't mind that I wrote about all our foibles and fantasies?"

Tun inhaled deeply. Her face shone.

"It was a great idea!"

"So you're not afraid your students and their parents will read the hot text message that I sent you at eight?"

"Honestly, I'd forgotten all about it," Tun said. "But what a wonderful memory. And what a wonderful message—sent in all innocence. I'm grateful to have recovered it."

"How about the CEO whose shareholders discover that he tried his own father?" I asked Hai.

"Every kid tries his parents," Hai said. "In every way," he added, laughing. "And parents sometimes need to know that they're on trial. He picked up a flowerpot and banged like a gavel. "All rise."

Ti was not at all surprised when I told her about my two visitors, and the surprise they gave me.

"I was in on it," she said, with a guilty smile.

"The stories would have been lost forever if you hadn't told them in a novel. They would have disappeared into the dusk, by the river, with their tails between their legs, like the dogs did."

"Are you better at cooking instant noodles now?" I asked her, embarrassed at how much I felt.

"What about you? Are *you* better at cooking them?"

Then she rummaged in her pocket. "I also have something for you to sign," she said.

"A cancelled ticket?" I stared at it blankly.

"Not cancelled—validated. Let's just say

it's a ticket on the train to childhood. Your book gave it to me, and I took the ride."

But you can, without a ticket, revisit your childhood any time. Just slip out of the shallow manmade canal and into the deep water.